THE BEST OF UNCLE ARTHUR'S

Bedtime
Stories

VOLUME TWO

The lighthouse children

Long ago on a rocky shore stood a lighthouse. Night after night its brilliant beam shone out across the dark and dangerous waters.

Slowly the light turned, growing brighter, then fainter, then brighter again, never failing, always warning of the rocks that lay beneath. Ships that passed in the night understood, and sailed in safety into the harbour.

Winter and summer the light blazed on. Through long, calm starlit nights, through storm and hurricane it never went out. The deeper the darkness the more brilliantly it shone; the more terrible the storm the more welcome were its warning beams.

In that far-off, lonely lighthouse lived a man, his wife, and two children, Paul and Rene. It was a quiet and strange life for them. Their home was the tall, narrow lighthouse. Their life centred in the light above them. They were there for one purpose – to keep the light burning.

One evening as dusk was falling, Father climbed up the steep, narrow staircase, as he had done so many times before, to light the lamp. In a few moments he returned, looking pale and sick.

'I'm ill', he said, and fell into a chair.

Mother ran over to him. She saw that he was very, very ill indeed. For a moment everything was confusion. Worried as they were, all Paul and Rene could do was stand and watch.

It would not be possible to contact a doctor till morning. After a struggle the lighthouse keeper closed his eyes and went into a deep sleep.

'Mother, what about the light?' Paul asked eventually.

'Go and see', she answered. 'I can't go now.'

So Paul and Rene crept softly out of the little room and climbed up the cold, dark staircase.

Night had fallen. A storm was blowing up, and dark clouds scudded across the pale moon. Below, great waves boomed on the rocks, the spray hissing as it fell back into the wild sea.

The light was burning, but there was something wrong. Over the sea everything was dark, and the great beam from the lighthouse shone only towards the land.

'Rene!' shouted Paul, 'The shade isn't turning. The ships will never see the light.'

'Can you start the machinery?' Rene called back.

'I'll try', answered Paul.

Paul had seen his father fix it many times and thought he could do it now. But he soon found that something was the matter; something had gone wrong. A piece of the machinery was broken and he could not mend it.

'What shall we do?' exclaimed Rene.

'There is the hand wheel left', said Paul.

'But you won't be able to turn that alone.'

'No, but we could turn it together', he answered.

'I'll help you', Rene volunteered.

Grabbing the great hand wheel they began to turn it. The shade of the light moved, much to their relief. The ships would see the light after all.

Hour after hour they worked. No night had ever seemed so long. Their hands became sore and blistered. Their arms grew tired. Minutes seemed like hours and hours like years. They grew so weary that they cried as they turned. Outside the storm broke and raged in fury around them. Below, Father was still in a deep sleep and Mother was very worried and longing for morning when the doctor could be called and brought over in a boat, weather permitting. Still the children of the lighthouse kept turning, turning, turning. Tired out, they carried on until a faint grey light in the east told them that their task was done.

Captains saw the light that night and thanked God for it. Later, in the newspaper, they found out what had been happening in the lighthouse, and the heroism of those two children.

Just as Paul and Rene kept the light turning through the long, stormy night, so God wants every child of His to keep the light of His love shining out into the cold, dark world. The darker our surroundings, the more brightly our light must shine. However bad the storm, our light must burn without a flicker. There are many ships passing, looking to us for comfort and guidance and friendliness. So we who are children of the light must keep it burning through the night.

When Danny ran away

Danny was upset again.

In fact, it seemed that he was always getting upset about something. If he did not get his own way all the time he would carry on in the most terrible manner. And if anyone told him off he would either snarl angrily or wander off into some corner and sulk.

When Danny was in these very bad moods he would mutter threats about running away from home. Although he was only 10 years old he had a very big opinion of himself and was quite sure he was able to look after himself 'out there'. The fact that he owed his father and mother anything at all for their loving care never seemed to enter his head. He only wanted to get away from all the rules, away to some place where he would be able to do just as he pleased.

Now he was thinking these thoughts again. Dad had asked him to cut the lawn just as he had planned to go out and play football with the boy next door. How he hated cutting the lawn! Why should he cut the lawn? He wished there were no lawn to cut. He would give anything to get away from the sight of it. But he did cut it, with anger almost bursting out of him.

That afternoon his plans were changed again.

Several times, in fact. As a result he became rude and cross and finished up with a good spanking and being sent to bed early. He did not say his prayers, and instead of going to sleep, began to plan his 'escape'. He would get up when everyone else had gone to bed, creep out of the house, and run far, far away. He was not quite sure where he woud go, or what he would do when he got there. He just wanted to get away where there would be no lawn to cut and where he wouldn't have to give up things for his brothers and sisters, nor be expected to do what he was told.

At last, when everything was still, and he felt sure that everyone must be fast asleep, he decided to put his plan into action.

He climbed softly out of bed, put on his clothes very quietly, took the money from his piggy bank, and crept out of his room.

As he passed the bed where his baby brother was lying asleep, he realized that he would never see little Jimmy again, so he bent over and kissed him; and a strange lump came into his throat so that he couldn't swallow very well. He kissed Jimmy twice and then went out of the room. Going past the room where Mum and Dad were asleep, he thought he would like to say goodbye, to Mum anyway. He wasn't quite sure about Dad, because he had made him cut the lawn. But, really, he didn't like the thought of not seeing Mum any more. He began to

wonder whether he should run away after all. Then the old, hard feeling came back and he went downstairs. Very quietly he put on his coat and gloves, unlocked the front door, and went out into the cold night air.

He stopped on the doorstep. This was hardly what he had dreamed about. It was too dark for one thing and too cold for another. Bed began to seem very nice. Perhaps, after all, it would be better to go back.

But no, he wouldn't. He closed the door. There was a snap! and he realized that he couldn't go back now even if he wanted to. That wasn't a nice feeling at all and he wished he hadn't let the door close quite so tightly.

It was closed now, though, so off he must go. He went down to the front gate and out into the road. There was nobody about. All was very quiet and still. The sky was black, and the only light came from the street lamps. It was all very eerie. Danny didn't like it a bit. If the door wasn't locked, he told himself, he would go back to bed.

He walked some distance down the road, and as the cold night air cooled him down, he began to realize more and more what a foolish plan he had started on. 'If the boys at school get to hear about this,' he said to himself, 'they'll tease me for the rest of term.' The very thought of his school friends discovering his foolishness made him turn round suddenly and make for home.

He had not gone far, however, when he nearly jumped out of his skin as a heavy hand was laid on his shoulder and a strange voice spoke to him.

'What are you doing out at this time of night?' asked the policeman.

Danny was frozen with fright. He had not expected this. Words would not come. He struggled to get free.

'You'd better come along with me', said the policeman. 'You've been up to some mischief, I'll bet.'

'I haven't, I haven't', gasped Danny. 'I've made a mistake, that's all.'

'I should think you have made a mistake, being out here at one o'clock in the morning. You can tell me all about it when we get down to the station.'

'You're not going to take me to the police station, are you!' cried Danny, more frightened still. 'Let me go home! I want to go home!'

'You'll go home, all right,' said the policeman, 'after we have had a little chat in the warm.'

And so poor Danny found himself for the first time in his life on his way to the police station!

There he was asked more questions in ten minutes than any teacher had ever asked him at school. Afterwards he was given a very rough mattress to lie on until the morning. He didn't sleep at all. He was too frightened, wondering what the

policeman was going to do with him and what his Dad would say. How he wished he had never started out on such a foolish adventure! How comfortable his own bed seemed. And there was no Jimmy to talk to when he woke up, and no Mum to come to him when he called. What a night it was!

Morning dawned at last. Very early the policeman came and told Danny to put his clothes on. Together they walked back home. How very small poor Danny felt! What a home-coming! What would the others say?

Dad, still in his pyjamas, opened the door.

'What in the world . . .' he began.

The policeman explained, and then with a smile went back to the station. Danny jumped into Dad's arms and hugged him, pyjamas and all. They didn't say much to each other, but just walked up the stairs like that to tell Mum all about it.

For breakfast that morning Mum gave everybody egg and toast in addition to their porridge, and she even opened a new pot of marmalade, because she said that as her little prodigal son had returned she had to 'kill the fatted calf', just like the story in the Bible.

And as for Danny, he said that he had run away for the last time in his life, and that he wouldn't be talking about doing so again!

A change of plan

The weather forecast said that snow was coming. This was good news for John and Gavin. Now was the time for some action!

They had often talked about making sledges for themselves, but so far had never done so. The good news about the snow made them decide to make one each. And with much excitement they began.

Every moment they could spare from their school work the boys spent in the shed at the bottom of the garden, sawing, planing, hammering, until the sledges were finished and ready for the snow when it came.

But it did not come. Probably the clouds were blown away after the weather experts had looked at them. Whatever happened it is certain that for many days there were two sledges in the garden and no snow to slide them on.

The school term ended, and still there was no snow. Day after day went by, cold and wet. There seemed about as much hope of snow as of a heat wave. The boys gave up, and wished they had never taken the trouble to make their sledges.

At last Christmas eve arrived and with it came a sudden change. The rain stopped, it grew cold all of a sudden, and a strong wind began to blow.

'Something is going to happen', said John, as he

went to bed that night. And he was right.

In the morning the clouds had gone and the rising sun glistened on a vast expanse of snow. A heavy fall had covered the whole landscape with a sparkling white coat.

John was overjoyed. As soon as he woke up he guessed what had happened. He could see the reflection of the snow on the ceiling. Leaping out of bed, he dressed as quickly as he could, and rushed down the garden to the shed where the sledges had been stored so long. With difficulty he hauled them both over the snow to the house, and then ran off to find Gavin.

This was even better than they had hoped for. No Christmas day could have started with so much excitement. They decided that they would go off at once to a nearby hill.

Off down the road they went, dragging their sledges behind them. School friends shouted after them: 'Let's have a ride?'

'No fear,' shouted the boys, 'we're going off by ourselves today.'

'Lend us one of your sledges', yelled another.

'You should have made one for yourself!' was John's reply.

Phil Morton, the disabled boy, waved his hand cheerfully from his window and wished them a great time.

'That was nice of him, wasn't it?' said Gavin.

'Yes,' said John, 'specially as he'll never be able to ride on a sledge of his own.'

Just then they passed Mandy Green's house. They had always been friendly with her and her little sisters. She greeted them cheerfully as usual, and wished them a happy Christmas.

'Wish I could come for a ride,' she said, 'but I can't this morning. I'm helping Mum round the house so that she can have a happy Christmas as well.'

The boys carried on. Soon they were out of the village and climbing the hill, dragging their sledges behind them. Then the fun began.

Swish! Away they went down the hill. Then they walked to the top again. Then another super slide. So they had fun together for a couple of hours.

After a while, however, John noticed a change coming over Gavin.

'What's up?' he asked as they climbed up the hill together.

'Nothing much,' said Gavin, 'only somehow I'm not having as much fun as I thought I would.'

'I'm not either,' admitted John. 'Of course, it's great, but I don't sort of feel comfortable. I wonder why it is?'

'Strange we should both feel the same way', said Gavin.

'Really strange', said John as they trudged on up to the top.

Swish! Down they went again.

On the way up again they talked about their strange feelings.

'I think I know what's up', said John.

'What?' asked Gavin.

'I keep thinking about Phil.'

'So do I', said Gavin. 'And Mandy and the others. I wish we hadn't left them behind. Bit mean, wasn't it?'

'Yes', said John.

There was silence again as they climbed slowly up the hill with their sledges.

'I think we'll have one more go', said John.

'All right', agreed Gavin.

They had their last ride, and then turned towards home. On the way they talked about how they would spend the afternoon, and when they reached the village they began calling at the homes of some of their friends who didn't have sledges. What they said seemed to make them very happy.

Dinner was hardly over when there was a loud knock at their front door. Running out, John and Gavin found a happy, excited group of children waiting for them.

'Hurray!' they all cried when they saw the two boys. 'I'm first', said one, and 'Me, me, me first!' called another.

Then, sorting the children out, John and Gavin put two or three of them on each of their sledges

and began to give them rides up and down the road. Oh, the shrieks of joy, the laughing and the yelling!

All afternoon they kept it up – except for a game of snowballs now and then – giving rides to all the children in turn, until at last, too weary to run any more, John and Gavin sent them all home and put the hard-worked sledges back in the shed.

'Well, it's been a super day,' said Gavin, 'but the afternoon was the best of all.'

'Yes, great!' said John, 'Fantastic! The morning on the hill wasn't anything like it!'

'You know, John,' said Gavin, 'I made up my mind I wouldn't let anyone use my sledge, but I didn't begin to enjoy it until I started to share it with the others.'

'You're right', said John. 'Doesn't the Bible say somewhere that "It is more blessed to give than to receive"? I think that's why we both felt so much happier after dinner, don't you?'

And Gavin agreed. 'This has been the best Christmas day we've ever had.'

Mischievous Maggie

Little Maggie was perhaps the most mischievous child who ever lived. She used to do the most dreadful things that any little girl could think up. You couldn't imagine the tricks she would play, and I hardly dare tell you about them. Once when she had lost her skipping rope, she went into the back garden when her mother was out shopping and, climbing onto one of the dining-room chairs, cut off a piece of the clothesline! What happened when Mother returned, I'm sure you don't want to hear.

Then one day – I must tell you about this – Daddy discovered Maggie sitting on the kitchen table 'cleaning' his shoes with black paint! Poor Daddy didn't know whether to laugh or be cross. However, as he loved his little girl very much, he told himself that probably Maggie thought she was trying to help. But the shoes never looked right again.

Another day she tried to find where the noise came from in the alarm clock. She managed to get the clock to pieces, but no one could ever put it together again!

There seemed no end to Maggie's mischief. It just bubbled out of her. Mummy and Daddy often wondered what would happen to her when she grew up. They didn't know what to do. But it turned out that Maggie cured herself.

Daddy had bought a new camera, and was very proud of it. But it was of more interest to Maggie than anyone else.

Almost before the camera was unpacked she wanted Daddy to take her picture. He said he couldn't possibly do it until the next morning. So Maggie was up early to have her picture taken. She was anxious to have a really good picture, as she wanted to show it to her friend next door, whose daddy had often taken *her* picture. She hoped that her picture would look prettier than that of her friend.

Well, Daddy took the photograph – in fact he took six of them, showing Maggie in all sorts of positions. Maggie was delighted, and looked forward to getting the prints.

Daddy went off to work and left the camera on his bedside table, telling Maggie that he would get the pictures developed when he returned.

But Maggie, mischievous as ever, could not wait so long for her pictures. She didn't see why she couldn't take them out of the camera just as well as Daddy; and he would be pleased to see them when he got home.

So Maggie sat down at the table and began to look at the camera. She didn't know how to open it but she pulled and pushed until at last her finger

accidentally touched a little button on the side and the back opened. Maggie was delighted, and felt sure she would now find her pictures. Inside was a long strip of queer-looking plastic. She pulled all this out, but still there seemed to be no pictures. The camera was empty.

Maggie was very disappointed, and felt sure Daddy must have made a mistake. Then she tried to put the plastic strip back inside so that Daddy would find it as he had left it; but somehow it wouldn't go, and the more she worked at it, the worse it became, and finally she gave up in despair.

Maybe you can guess what happened when Daddy got back from work.

Anyhow, after Maggie had stopped crying, Daddy explained to her how she had spoiled all his pictures, and that she could never see the ones he had taken that morning – and that they were all on that queer-looking strip of plastic waiting to be developed, but because of her impatience, they would never be seen by anyone.

Maggie was so disappointed she said that she would never do it again, and that after this she really would try to be good. And while she did not always keep her promise, it is a fact that the lesson she learned that day remained with her ever after.

Caught by the tide

I have told many stories about all sorts of boys and girls that perhaps it is time I told one about myself.

In my Bible, beside a certain text, are written three words – 'North Uist Ford' – and every time I look at them they remind me of the most exciting adventure I have ever had.

Many years ago when I was 15 years old, I decided to go to college. To do this I had to earn a lot of money to pay my fees. To earn the money I took a job selling books from door to door.

They didn't seem to worry much about my age, and sent me to the Outer Hebrides, far-away islands off the west coast of Scotland. Here I soon found myself, quite alone, cycling around barren, wind-swept islands, trying my best to interest people in the books I carried with me.

First of all I tried the island of Lewis. I cycled for miles without a house in sight, and sometimes with rain and wind beating in my face all the way. I travelled a little further each day until I had worked right up to the lighthouse on the most northerly point. The lighthouse-keeper was very kind. I remember him because he bought a book from me!

After doing all I could on the island of Lewis I went by boat down to the next island, called North Uist, and found lodgings in a little thatched cottage, where the rats played round my bed at night. Everything was so old fashioned that I remember telling the lady that I didn't think the people were civilized there yet – didn't I get into trouble!

There is a circular road on this island and I cycled and trudged all round it, going to places where I am sure no lad of my age had ever tried to sell books before.

At last I had sold all the books I could on this island, and wondered where to go next. So I began to explore southwards, having been told that I could cross to the next large island by walking across the fords at low tide. I thought this would be a good idea as it would save me the expense of taking the ferry.

Going down to the first ford one morning I looked over it very carefully. The tide was out and from a distance it seemed that all I had to do was walk across the sand to a tiny island and from there, across more sand, to where I wanted to be. But as I drew nearer I realized it was not going to be quite as easy as that. Running through the sand were channels of water, some of them very wide. How deep they were I didn't know. Anyhow, I could see that I would have to take my shoes and socks off and wade at least part of the way.

Just then I saw two men begin to cross, and watched them for some minutes, making sure I remembered the places where they waded through

27

the channels. I noticed, too, that they were hurrying, but didn't understand why. I just thought they had some urgent business on the other side. But there was a stronger reason than that.

Taking off my shoes and socks, tying the laces together, and slinging them around my neck, I began to follow them. Crossing the first channel was easy. I remembered exactly where the men had gone over, and the water was only a few inches deep. But when I reached the second, I was not quite so sure of my position and found that the channel was much deeper than I had expected. I rolled my trousers up over my knees, but I still couldn't make it. Not too worried, I walked up and down the sand till I saw where I could cross in safety.

When I reached the third channel, however, which was about the middle of the crossing from island to island, I began to feel a bit scared. It was much larger than when I had first looked at it. Even then the terrible truth had not dawned on me. Perhaps, if I had been older, I might have understood what a dangerous thing I was trying to do, but I didn't know, and there was no one to tell me.

By this time I had forgotten the place where the men had crossed and tried here and there to find the shallow water. But I couldn't find any.

Then it dawned on me that the water was no longer still, as it had been. It was moving, and quite

rapidly at that. Bits of seaweed, pieces of wood, and sea foam, were floating by – the tide was coming in!

I looked back, and I'll never forget what I saw. Instead of a wide stretch of sand there was a vast waste of water. It seemed that the whole Atlantic Ocean was rolling in on me.

The island of sand on which I stood was rapidly becoming smaller and smaller. Every moment the channel beside me was getting deeper and deeper. Within a few minutes the place where I stood would be many feet below the surface of the water. I knew I must act immediately, or be swept away by the fierce, onrushing tide.

But what could I do? If I did not know the way when the channel was shallow, how could I find it now when it had become already twice as deep and was spreading out over the sand in every direction?

Yet somehow, even in that most desperate situation, I felt sure God would see me through. There was no time for long prayers. Every moment counted. I remember asking Him to guide me as, taking my courage in both hands, I plunged into the water.

It was no use trying to save my trousers now. The water came above my knees, above my waist, higher and higher. Would my feet ever stop going down? For a moment I wondered if I had made a mistake. Should I go back and try to find my way back through the channels I had crossed? But looking behind showed that that was now impossible. Everywhere the sand was covered. No one could find the channels now.

Deeper and deeper – was this the end?

And then I realized that the ground was beginning to rise again. I must be half-way through! The water was becoming more shallow.

There were still some other channels to cross though. How I found my way through them I don't know. I can still remember it. With water above my waist, I was wandering here and there, searching with my feet for the shallow places, while all the time I could see the waters from the Atlantic surging in around me.

I did find my way – or I would not be writing this story now – and at last I crawled out on to the island towards which I had set out so confidently half an hour before. I leave you to imagine how I looked with all my clothes dripping wet. What a sight I was! If there had been any children around I'm sure they would have laughed.

An old man came up and told me – as if I didn't know it! – what a narrow escape I had had. He had been watching me all the time and never expected to see me get over alive. He kindly found someone with a boat who took me back to where I had started out, and I returned to my lodgings to dry my clothes and thank God for delivering me.

Now you will understand why I have marked that

text in my Bible. It is found in the forty-third chapter of Isaiah, the second and third verses. I can't help but feel it was written for me, for this is how it reads:

'When you pass through deep waters, I am with you, when you pass through rivers, they will not sweep you away; . . . for I am the Lord your God, the Holy One of Israel, your deliverer.'

Bonfire night

It was the fifth of November. For many weeks the children had been collecting all sorts of rubbish and piling it up in the garden for the great bonfire night. There was now a large heap of sticks, boxes, old newspapers, broken doors, and many other odds and ends that would burn well.

'Dad, can we have some fireworks?' begged Andrew for the ninety-ninth time that morning.

'I don't think we should spend money on fireworks at the moment', said Dad. 'As I've told you before . . .'

'But, Dad,' chorused the rest, 'just a few! A few won't hurt anybody, and it won't seem right without just one or two.'

'All right', sighed Dad. 'I suppose I shall have to get some, after all.'

'Good old Dad! Some bangers, and Roman candles, and rockets, and . . .'

'I said a few!'

'All right, then, we'll leave it to you.'

'Well,' said Dad, 'if I do get a few it's on condition that there'll be no quarrelling over them.'

'Oh, that's all right', they all said together. 'We won't quarrel. We never do!'

'Oh, no?' said Dad. 'Of course you don't. I think I've heard that story before. We'll wait and see.'

At last night fell and the great moment all the children had been longing for arrived. But no Dad appeared and, of course, no fireworks.

'It's too bad', said Andrew. 'He should have brought them.'

As the minutes passed and Dad did not come, they became more and more impatient. At last Andrew said he was going to light the fire anyway. He struck a match and in an instant there was a great roar as the flames leapt up. It was a great sight, but somehow it wasn't the same without Dad.

'Why hasn't Dad come?' asked one, then another, as they all got more and more upset. 'Why hasn't he brought the fireworks? Why is he spoiling everything like this?'

The fire was already dying down when someone shouted, 'Here he is!'

Sure enough, here was Dad – who had been delayed at the office on important business – running down the garden with a waste-paper basket full of fireworks in his arms.

But he didn't get a very warm welcome.

'Why have you come so late?' asked Andrew.

'You've spoiled everything', said another.

'The fireworks won't be any good now', said a third.

'Well!' exclaimed Dad. 'I think I'll take them away again!'

34

'No, don't do that!' cried Andrew, seizing one of the Roman candles from the basket in a very rude, bad-tempered way and trying to set it alight.

'Andrew,' said Dad firmly, 'what did I tell you . . .'

But Dad did not finish his sentence. The Roman candle was already alight and throwing up a shower of golden rain followed by green and red stars that soared up into the darkness.

Suddenly there was a loud Bang!

But the noise did not come from the Roman candle. Everyone turned to the basket.

A spark from the candle, which had been placed too near the basket, had fallen on the fuse of one of the large crackers. But worse was to follow.

Bang! Bang! Bang!

The first explosion had smothered the other crackers with sparks and now it seemed that all were going off at once.

'Turn them out of the basket!' shrieked someone. But it was too late. Quicker than they could act, a flame had shot up and set basket and all on fire.

What a sight it was! Red fire and green fire mingling together, and stars of various colours leaping into the air and spraying themselves around in all directions.

Crack! crack! crack! went the jumping-jacks, jumping all over the place.

Bang! Bang! Bang! went the big bangers.

Whizz! went a sky rocket right past Andrew's head.

It was all over in less than three minutes and then all that was left was the bottom of the waste-paper basket and a group of very sad and disappointed children.

'Well, it was pretty while it lasted', said Dad, trying to be cheerful.

'If only you had come earlier . . .' began Andrew crossly.

'Yes, and if only you had not been so impatient', said Dad. 'Never, NEVER try to light fireworks yourselves. Every year on bonfire night there are terrible accidents. Some children are blinded. Others have their faces badly burned. Some are even killed.'

It was a sorry little party that filed up the garden, and Dad's heart melted at the sight of their tearful faces.

By a strange coincidence he found some pound coins at the bottom of his trouser pocket and set off with the boys to the corner shop just before it closed. So they had 'a few' fireworks after all. But the lesson of that evening was not forgotten. For whenever any of them was tempted to be cross or impatient after that he thought of the terrible night when all the fireworks went off at once.

Just-a-minute Janet

'Janet! Janet!' called Mummy.

No reply.

'Coo-ee! Janet!' she called again, going to the kitchen window to see what Janet was doing.

'Just a minute, Mummy', came a little voice from the garden. 'I won't be long.'

'But I'm waiting for you', called Mummy. 'I want you to come now.'

'Just a minute', came floating back from the invisible Janet.

'Oh, dear!' exclaimed Mummy to herself. 'How tired I am of hearing her say, "Just a minute". Just wait till she comes in!'

Five minutes passed. Then ten minutes. But no Janet appeared.

'Janet!' called Mummy, going to the window again. 'Come here at once!'

'Just a minute!'

'Oh!' said Mummy. 'If you don't . . .'

But at that moment Janet's little face popped round the corner of the toolshed, smiling so sweetly that Mummy didn't know what to say next.

'Here I am', said Janet brightly. 'Did you call, Mummy?'

'You heard me call', said Mummy, trying to look stern. 'Why didn't you come at once?'

'I was busy', replied Janet. 'You see, I was washing dolly's clothes.'

'Maybe you were,' said Mummy, 'but when I call you must obey at once. It's very rude to keep me waiting ten whole minutes before you come.'

'Yes, Mummy', said Janet.

'And don't you ever say, "Just a minute" again.'

'No, Mummy.'

'All right,' said Mummy, 'now take these eggs round to Mrs. Jones.'

Janet took the box and ran off happily, humming a little tune to herself. But while she was gone she quite forgot all that Mummy had said.

When she returned she went out into the garden again to her 'wash-tub' behind the shed. What fun it was rubbing and scrubbing and making soap-suds. And she had a clothes' line all to herself, and some of Mummy's pegs too. No wonder she was happy!

But by and by she heard a familiar voice again.

'Janet! Janet! Dinner time!'

The reply was equally familiar too.

'Just a minute, Mummy!'

'So she has forgotten already', said Mummy. 'Then she will have to learn some other way.'

Once more the minutes passed – five minutes, ten minutes, fifteen minutes. Still no sign of Janet.

But meanwhile Mummy went on eating her dinner and when she had finished, she started to clear the table. Just then an unusual sound caught her ears.

'Mummy! Mummy! Come quick! Come quick! The water's spilled all over me!'

Suddenly a bright idea came to Mummy. Feeling sure that nothing serious had happened, she called out:

'Just a minute, Janet!'

'Oh, come quick! come quick!' wailed Janet; 'my shoes are full of water!'

But Mummy finished clearing the table, calling back once more:

'Just a minute, Janet!'

At this, Janet, soaked through, appeared round the corner. What a picture she looked! She had jumped off the stool after hanging dolly's frock on her washing line and had brought the whole basin full of soapy water on top of herself.

Mummy couldn't help laughing. It was too funny for words.

'Why didn't you come when I called?' said Janet very crossly. 'Can't you see I'm all wet?'

'I couldn't', said Mummy. 'You see, I was busy. I had to clear the table after dinner.'

'Is it as late as that?' asked Janet, looking surprised.

'Yes', said Mummy. 'And I've been waiting for you all this time. If you had come when I called this wouldn't have happened.'

Janet saw the point and a faint little smile flickered across her face. And, of course, that was the end of it. Mummy ran to get her some dry clothes *and* some dinner, while Janet promised once more that she would never keep Mummy waiting again.

Curious Katie's custard cake

Little Katie was very much the same as other little girls of her age; just about as tall, just about as broad, and just about as pretty. But those who knew her best knew that there was one particular difference. *All* little girls of 8 years of age are very curious, but Katie seemed to be very, *very* curious.

One afternoon during the Christmas holidays, Katie was helping her mother in the kitchen. She always liked to do this when Mummy was cooking.

This particular afternoon Katie seemed more curious than ever. She wanted to look first in one thing, then in another. Every now and then she would put her finger into the mixtures Mummy was making just to 'see what they tasted like'.

At last Mummy became tired of Katie's mischief and sent her out to one of the nearby shops.

With Katie out of the way Mummy soon got through her work. When she had done her cooking she thought she would prepare something nice as a special treat for Katie, as two of her friends were coming to have tea with her that evening.

Taking one of the small sponge cakes she had just made, she cut it in two, put some strawberry jam inside, and then poured over it a custard she had made in the morning. Then she put some pieces of banana and one or two bright red cherries on top, and when it was finished it really did look very nice indeed. So that it would be a surprise at tea-time, Mummy put the dish in one of the kitchen cupboards out of sight.

After a while Katie returned, still as curious as ever. She wanted to know what her mother had been making while she had been away. Then she peered into the oven to see if anything was still being cooked. As the oven was empty she guessed that most of the things would be in the fridge or one of the cupboards. She was just trotting across to the cupboard where the surprise had been hidden when her mother called to her:

'Katie, you are not to open that cupboard.'

'But I want to see what you've made.'

'You must not open it', said Mother firmly.

Katie reluctantly turned away. She was really curious now. What could there be in that cupboard? Surely something really nice. Longing to open the door, she moved slowly towards it again.

'Katie!'

Katie knew what that meant. Again she walked away.

'But, Mummy, what's in there?' she asked.

'Never mind; it is something nice for you and the other girls to have for tea.'

'But can't I look? Just *one* look, Mummy?'

'No.'

Just then the next door neighbour called over the garden wall, asking Mother to come and see her baby who was sick.

With a last warning to Katie that she was not to touch either the fire or the cupboard, Mother hurried away to help her neighbour.

Katie sat on a chair and looked longingly at the forbidden cupboard. What could be behind those closed doors?

'I wonder if Mummy would mind if I had just one peep?' she said to herself. But Mother's last warning was still in her mind. However, she continued to look at the cupboard, and longed for the doors to open.

'Just one peep', she kept thinking. 'Only one.'

She got off the chair and walked towards the cupboard.

A tempting voice seemed to whisper in her ear, 'Just pull open the door and you'll see.'

The nearer Katie got to the cupboard the stronger became the temptation. She dragged a chair up, stood on it, and began to pull the door open. The hinges creaked rather noisily, and she looked round sharply to see if her mother was coming, but no one was about.

When the door was open about three inches, Katie looked in. Ah, there it was, on the bottom shelf, right in front. How beautiful it looked! She

opened the door a little wider. Being rather a heavy one, it slipped out of her fingers and swung wide open.

What a lovely sight that dish was. Katie bent forward to smell it. 'It must taste nice', she thought, and, stretching out a hand, she touched it. What lovely custard! She had another taste.

Just then a slight noise close at hand caused her to turn round suddenly. She couldn't see anything that might have caused the noise, but she felt sure that something had touched her. Frightened, she hurriedly closed the door and sat down again.

Hardly had she done so when Mother returned. Katie tried to look as innocent as possible, and Mother did not suspect that anything was wrong. Together they cleared up the kitchen and washed the dishes. When it was done, Katie brought out her tea things and arranged them on the table ready for her two friends.

It was almost five o'clock and the other children would soon be arriving.

'Would you like to see what is in the cupboard now, Katie?' asked her mother.

'Yes, please', said Katie, rather sheepishly, and looking very uncomfortable.

Mother wondered what was the matter, but said nothing.

'Well, dear, you may open the cupboard now if you like. The others will soon be here.'

Katie walked across the room, and, just as she had done a little earlier in the afternoon, climbed onto a chair to open the cupboard door. As she did so she uttered a cry of dismay.

'Mummy! There's nothing here.'

'What!' exclaimed Mother.

Mother ran across the room and looked in. It was true. Where she had put the pretty custard sponge cake earlier there was nothing but an unsightly mess at the bottom of the glass dish.

'Katie! have you touched this?' asked Mother sorrowfully.

Katie was crying now.

'No – er – yes – er – well – I didn't eat it. I didn't really, but – I did look in – oh, dear, what has happened?' sobbed Katie.

Just then Mummy noticed a low purring noise coming from the other end of the cupboard, and putting in her hand she grabbed – the cat.

'Katie, how could you have been so naughty?' she asked.

'But I didn't put the cat in – it must have jumped in by itself – when – when I opened the door, before – oh, dear!' sighed Katie.

It might not be wise or pleasant to describe all that happened during the next few minutes. Let's just say that Katie's curiosity was reduced to normal, and the three girls had a very plain tea of bread, butter and jam.

Ken's baby brother

For five whole years Ken had been the centre of attention in the house. As he was the only little boy, Mummy and Daddy had no one else to love but him. They had loved him such a lot and paid so much attention to him that he had come to think that he was 'the only pebble on the beach'.

Then one day something happened. Ken came into the house after playing in the garden to find the whole place upside down, with strange people bustling about and generally taking charge of things. He was told to be very good and quiet and to keep out of the way, because a little baby brother had just arrived.

Ken didn't know what to do. He had been told a baby was coming but now it had all happened so suddenly and so mysteriously. Of course he wanted to see the new baby very much, but he had to wait as patiently as he could for a long time before he was allowed to do so.

At first Ken felt very proud that he had a baby brother, and took great pleasure and pride in describing him in detail to his friends. But as the days went by, Ken's delight in the new baby began to disappear. Very soon he noticed that Mummy was spending much more time on the baby than on him. Little things he had always expected Mummy to do for him he now had to do himself. In the morning, for instance, there seemed to be so many things for Mummy to do for the baby that Ken had to dress himself and tie his own shoe-laces. He didn't like it a bit.

In his mind Ken began to blame the baby for the change, and now and then, when Mummy asked him to help her by doing some little job, perhaps setting the table or sweeping up the crumbs, he would say he wished the baby had never been born.

Ken, too, had always been used to receiving all the presents that came to the house. There had been no one else to have any. But now he found people bringing pretty things for the baby and not noticing him. 'You would think that I wasn't here', said Ken. As the months rolled by, Ken became more and more unhappy.

'Ken,' said Mother one day, 'don't you love your baby brother?'

'No', snapped Ken.

'But why? He has never done you any harm, and you will be able to play together when he grows up. Why don't you love him?'

'Everybody makes such a fuss of him – and they don't love me – and he takes all my toys and breaks them – and he cries such a lot – and I just don't like him.'

'But suppose something should happen to him

and you lost him, would you be sorry then?'

Ken hesitated, for he had just a little bit of love somewhere inside for the bright-eyed, fair-haired little dumpling that crawled around the house.

'Dunno', he said, and walked away to avoid giving an answer.

'I wish I could do something to make Ken love his little baby brother', said Mother to herself. But just then she couldn't think of anything to do. Ken's love was soon to be tested, however.

Next day was washday. Mother had left baby brother asleep in his cot up in the bedroom while she went on with her work. Ken was in the dining room building a garage with Lego, and Mummy had gone into the garden to hang out the clothes.

Just then, Ken heard a gentle thud on the floor above and then softer, little thuds followed.

'That baby has crawled out of his cot again!' he said to himself. 'I'd better go and see.'

But Ken was just finishing his garage and he thought it was safe to wait a few minutes before going up. Then he heard a strange sound.

Bumpity – bumpity – bumpity – bang! Bumpity – bump – bump – bump – bang!

Ken sprang to his feet and rushed out into the hall. There at the bottom of the stairs lay little brother. He had fallen down the whole fifteen steps from top to bottom.

'Mummy!' shrieked Ken, but Mummy, out in the

garden, didn't hear. So he ran to baby brother and picked him up.

'Poor little thing', he cried, hugging him tight. 'Wake up! Please don't die. I really don't want you to die. I *will* love you if you just wake up again.'

Just then baby brother gave a big cry, and the tears began to come. For the first time Ken was glad to hear him cry, and he cuddled him closer.

A few minutes later Mother came in, and you can imagine how surprised she was at who she found sitting on the bottom step in the hall.

Tom's thoughtlessness

It was a half-term holiday and Tom was spending it with some of his school friends in the park.

They had all brought lunchboxes, and after playing lots of games they sat down under an old oak tree to enjoy the good things their mothers had packed up for them.

After they had finished, for want of something better to do they began throwing the banana skins and orange peel at each other and scattering paper all over the place.

All of a sudden from behind the oak tree came an elderly gentleman. He went to walk past the boys, but, stepping on one of the banana skins, fell heavily to the ground.

Tom jumped up and did his best to help him to his feet again.

'I hope you're not hurt', he said.

'I don't think so', said the gentleman. 'Just a little shaken. I think I'll sit on your seat for a little while if that's all right.'

Tom helped him across to the seat and the boys stood around to see if he had hurt himself or not.

'I think I'm all right,' he said, 'but I'm getting on now and a fall like that is dangerous for someone my age. It's too bad that people are so careless with their banana skins, isn't it?'

'Yes', said Tom, but with rather a guilty look at the other boys.

'I hope you boys never throw banana skins about.'

'Um', said Tom, blushing a little.

'So selfish, isn't it?' went on the elderly gentleman.

'I suppose it is', said Tom.

'If people only thought of the pain they might cause others I'm sure they wouldn't do it.'

'No', said Tom.

'And look at all that paper lying about', said the elderly gentleman. 'Some lazy, thoughtless people must have been here.'

'Yes,' said Tom; there was nothing else he could say.

'If only', went on the gentleman, 'if only people would stop to think about others they would never leave a mess like this behind them, would they?'

'No', said Tom, getting more uncomfortable.

'You know,' said the gentleman, 'this is a beautiful park, and if everyone left a mess like this it wouldn't be worth coming to. If it were all covered with dirty paper and orange peel and banana skins you boys wouldn't want to play here, would you?'

'No fear', said Tom and the rest together.

'Well, boys, I'm feeling better now. Thank you for helping me up. I'll be off again, I think. Here's something for you to get some sweets.'